Dear Parents,

Welcome to the Scholastic Reader series. We have taken over 80 years of experience with teachers, parents, and children and put it into a program that is designed to match your child's interests and skills.

Level 1— Short sentences and stories made up of words kids can sound out using their phonics skills and words that are important to remember.

Level 2 — Longer sentences and stories with words kids need to know and new "big" words that they will want to know.

Level 3 — From sentences to paragraphs to longer stories, these books have large "chunks" of texts and are made up of a rich vocabulary.

Level 4 — First chapter books with more words and fewer pictures.

It is important that children learn to read well enough to succeed in school and beyond. Here are ideas for reading this book with your child:

- Look at the book together. Encourage your child to read the title and make a prediction about the story.
- Read the book together. Encourage your child to sound out words when appropriate. When your child struggles, you can help by providing the word.
- Encourage your child to retell the story. This is a great way to check for comprehension.
- Have your child take the fluency test on the last page to check progress.

Scholastic Readers are designed to support your child's efforts to learn how to read at every age and every stage. Enjoy helping your child learn to read and love to read.

— **Francie Alexander**
Chief Education Officer
Scholastic Education

To Vilma, Marcia, and Andrea, the coolest sisters
— S.B.

For Evelyne
— T.M.

Text copyright © 1999 by Sonia W. Black.
Illustrations copyright © 1999 by Turi MacCombie.
Activities copyright © 2003 Scholastic Inc.
All rights reserved. Published by Scholastic Inc.
SCHOLASTIC, CARTWHEEL BOOKS, and associated logos
are trademarks and/or registered trademarks of Scholastic Inc.

Library of Congress Cataloging-in-Publication Data is available.

ISBN: 0-439-09832-7

10 9 8

07

Printed in the U.S.A. 23 • First printing, November 1999

Plenty of Penguins

by **Sonia W. Black**
Illustrated by **Turi MacCombie**

Scholastic Reader — Level 1

SCHOLASTIC INC.
New York Toronto London Auckland Sydney
Mexico City New Delhi Hong Kong Buenos Aires

What's black and white
and cute as can be?

A penguin.
That's me.
Do you want to meet
my family?

Penguins are big.

And penguins are small.
We have sharp,
pointy feathers.
But that's not all....

We can have stripes.

or spots
here and there.

Long, bushy brows...

or spiky hair.

There are even bright colors
that some of us share.

I live at the South Pole.
It is covered with
ice,
    ice,
        ice.
I think ice is very nice.

We have homes
in other places, too —

South Africa,
New Zealand,
Australia,
and Peru.

We cannot fly
up,
   up,
      up, and away.
That is strange for a bird,
wouldn't you say?

We waddle and hop
and have lots of fun.
We swim.
And we dive
down
        deep,
            one by one.

We find many little fish,
squid, and shrimp
to eat.

They are mmm, mmm good.
Yum, yum – what a treat!

But we have to watch out.
We might become meals
for killer whales
and leopard seals.

On land
we live in great, big groups
called colonies.

They are also known
as rookeries.

We make nests.
We rest.

We lay eggs.
We keep them warm.

We watch,
and we wait,
and we keep them from harm
until…

The eggs hatch!

Hooray! Hooray!
New baby penguin chick
are here to stay.

Can you find these penguins in your book?

Adelie
penguin

Emperor
penguin

Fairy penguin
(also called
Little Blue)

Chinstrap
penguin

Magellan
penguin

Gentoo
penguin

roni
uin

Rockhopper
penguin